RUNNING
on a Patchwork
of EARTH

JONNY ZUCKER

A & C BLACK
AN IMPRINT OF BLOOMSBURY
LONDON NEW DELHI NEW YORK SYDNEY

CONTENTS

Chapter 1	A Patchwork of Earth	7
Chapter 2	Home of Champions	14
Chapter 3	The Race	22
Chapter 4	This is London	31
Chapter 5	First Day	38
Chapter 6	Tinnison	47
Chapter 7	Running Round in Circles	55
Chapter 8	A Unexpected Offer	62
Chapter 9	In Training	69
Chapter 10	A Chance to Run	79
Chapter 11	Father and Son	86
Chapter 12	Meeting Mum and Dad	94
Chapter 13	Beating the Wind	103

CHAPTER 1

A PATCHWORK OF EARTH

It's only 5.30 am!' protested Musa croakily, as his best mate, AK, threw off his bed sheets and grabbed him by the elbow. 'Are you completely crazy?'

'You're the one who's crazy!' laughed AK.

He pulled his friend out of bed and onto the cold stone floor of the dorm.

'Couldn't we go in half an hour?' pleaded Musa, looking longingly at his warm bed and at all of the other boys who were still sleeping.

AK and Musa were boarders at St Patrick's School for Boys in Iten, Kenya. They were the only people in the building who were awake.

'In an hour the whole place will be flooded with Olympic wannabes who'll be able to spy on my unique running style and our top-class fitness programme,' replied AK. 'If they steal our secrets we'll only have ourselves to blame!'

Musa sighed wearily, and swapped his pyjamas for running shorts and vest. 'As a tired human, I resent this early morning intrusion,' he said to AK, as they tiptoed out of the dorm. 'But as your business manager, I suppose there might be wisdom in your actions.'

They went down two flights of stairs and exited the school building. AK took a great lungful of air and blew it out. He shielded his eyes from the early morning sun settling over the Great Rift Valley, a section of the East African Rift that starts in Tanzania to the south and continues towards Ethiopia in the north. The hard-packed ochre-coloured earth glinted in the sun's rays and seemed to be calling out to AK.

It's time to run. It's time to climb another notch on the ladder to greatness!

'Let's go!' cried AK, pushing off along the path bordering the school. He wanted to shout for joy as his legs and feet clicked into rhythm and his chest burst into life like an old boiler given a service. The boys' bare feet pounded over the hard ground, and at the end of the path they joined another, this one snaking through several twists and turns. They ran on in silence until the path started rising and their bodies adjusted to the uphill trajectory.

'If only Kipketer or Rudisha could see us now!' said AK. 'I bet they'd be cheering us on.'

Wilson Kipketer (Gold in the 1995, 1997 and 1999 World Championships) and David Rudisha (Gold in the 2012 Olympics and the 2011 World Championships) were AK's heroes, both 800-metre specialists. That was AK's race, so their inspiration constantly fuelled his running ambitions.

'Maybe they'd buy us a flash car!' responded Musa. He was running at AK's side but while AK's breathing was calm and regular, Musa was finding the run a little more taxing.

'What would be the point of getting a car when we can't even drive?' enquired AK.

'We could store it in the garage they'd get for us!'

AK grinned at his friend's mad dreams. No matter what happened, Musa could always make him laugh.

As they ran on their strides propelled them to a height of seven thousand feet above sea level, yet they were still some way from the peak of the mountain. They entered a forest of juniper trees that towered above them, their broccoli-like leaf clusters perched on top of sturdy wide trunks. The junipers always made AK think of beefy wrestlers and he wouldn't have been surprised if two of the trees had jumped forward and challenged each other to a bout in the ring.

Higher and higher they climbed, AK's calf muscles feeling the familiar pull, one of the many bodily tensions you had to run through if you ever wanted to be a truly great athlete. Having a good running style was of course important, but possessing cauldrons of strength and stamina were equally crucial.

'For every race, you need to keep something back,' Brother Colm, the St Patrick's athletics coach, was forever telling AK and the other running hopefuls. 'Every middle distance champion can pull a sprint out of the bag at any time.'

AK might need to pull a sprint out of the bag this very day. Brother Colm would be holding running trials straight after school. Boys who were selected would be on the running team for the first inter-schools tournament of the season. AK was determined to be among the names on that teamsheet.

Ten minutes later Musa demanded a break. AK stopped reluctantly, and the two of them walked past several trees to the very edge of the mountain.

'Refreshment is needed.' Musa took a slug from a bottle of water he produced from the pocket of his running shorts. When he'd finished he passed the bottle to AK, who had a long drink. Their breaths per minute gradually reduced as their bodies responded to the stop. They looked down at the town of Iten below, with its two famous red arches.

Iten had just four thousand inhabitants but attracted such media interest that everyone at St Patrick's was well used to seeing TV crews and journalists swarming over the streets and around the school (when allowed), looking for famous and up-and-coming runners to interview, and seeking out new training methods to report on. And all of them, every single one, wanted to interview Brother Colm.

Beyond the town and stretching out to the south, the land sloped downwards into the Uasin-Gishu plateau, a fertile area dotted with cow and sheep farms and large areas of maize and wheat crops. It was like a patchwork of earth that had been specially arranged for their viewing pleasure.

'Do you really think that all of this extra early morning running is going to increase your chances of making it?' Musa asked, hands on hips.

AK said nothing but he was sure Musa could read the answer on his face.

AK was single-minded about running, a fact often mentioned by his teachers. 'If only AK applied himself to geography/maths/history as much as he did to running…' was the most frequent phrase in his school reports. AK's parents supported his athletics ambitions, but they were also keen for him to keep up with his schoolwork.

'If you don't make it as a runner you'll need a proper career to fall back on,' his scientist father was always telling him.

'Look at me,' said his midwife mother. 'My skills are transferable to anywhere in the world. If running doesn't happen, you'll also need a set of skills.'

As AK looked down on the plateau, the words of his parents drifted through his mind. He understood why they went on about schoolwork, but couldn't they see that running came miles above everything else? *Not* becoming a runner wasn't an option for him. He felt as if he had been placed on earth to be an internationally famous 800-metre world champion.

It wasn't just something he wanted to do. It was his destiny.

CHAPTER 2

HOME OF CHAMPIONS

AK had been right. By the time he and Musa had circled and run back down to the main road the whole place was crowded with runners, jostling for position as they pounded the tarmac. It was a daily ritual for hundreds, both young and old, to run under the red metal arch saying: WELCOME TO ITEN – HOME OF CHAMPIONS and down the main road until they passed under the other metal arch stating: THANKS FOR VISITING ITEN – HOME OF CHAMPIONS.

'I told you it was worth getting up early,' grinned AK. 'That lot will never develop a proper running style.'

'You're right,' nodded Musa, eyeing the herd. 'They're too busy stepping on each others' toes.'

The boys laughed as they walked back to St Patrick's. At the front of the building was a low brick wall carrying the school motto: EXCELLENCE IN ALL ENDEAVOURS.

'Apart from an endeavor called Maths,' muttered Musa. AK grinned and nodded his agreement.

They entered the building, went back up to their dorm and grabbed a shower. By the time they'd finished breakfast in the school canteen, the whole building was a bustling hive of activity. Boys were getting books out of lockers, looking in backpacks for much-needed items, and chatting and joking around with each other. A few students nodded hellos to AK and Musa and they responded with handshakes and backslaps.

When the day's lessons began, AK tried to focus on what the teachers were saying but his mind kept drifting off to the after-school running trials. Did he have enough to beat the other 800-metre runners? Would he lose to his arch-rival, Fumo – the most annoying boy in their year? What would he do if he didn't make the team?

He got told off for daydreaming in science, and would have missed answering an important question in history if it hadn't been for Musa nudging him in the ribs.

As soon as the bell went for the end of school AK raced to the changing rooms and got into his yellow running shorts and running top, and light blue trainers. He stepped out into the afternoon's sunshine and saw Brother Colm by the side of the track: the man who had the power to completely change AK's life.

To claim that Brother Colm was a legend was something of an understatement. He'd arrived at St Patrick's in 1976, intending to stay for three months as a geography teacher. But the intoxicating excitement and enthusiasm of the place had enveloped him and he'd never left. Teaching athletics hadn't been part of his plan at all, but the school coach Brother Peter Foster sought his help and together they started a running revolution. Brother Peter had since gone, but having trained a huge number of world champions and Olympic medallists, it was safe to say that Brother Colm knew a thing or two about running.

At that moment Brother Colm, dressed in black trousers and short-sleeved white shirt, with sunglasses and a grey baseball cap, was talking to two boys in the year above. AK jogged a short distance away and began to do some stretches, warming up his joints and muscles for the race ahead. As he did these he repeated his mantra in his head:

I am a runner. I have speed. I can beat the wind.

It was a phrase he'd thought up last spring and he'd stuck with it.

'Go, AK!' shouted Musa, who was sitting by the side of a track and keeping an eye on his friend's preparations.

AK grinned and waved.

'OK, boys!' called Brother Colm, beckoning the runners to join him.

There were about sixty boys in all and they stood huddled in a group.

'I need to whittle you lot down into an athletics team for our first race meet of the season,' announced the coach. 'Twelve of you will be selected. Don't worry if you don't get chosen. As I'm sure you know, there'll be plenty of other race days.'

The boys exchanged nervous looks.

'First place in each heat will make it onto the team,' said Brother Colm, 'and I'll ask several of you to run in more than one heat, OK?'

AK felt his heartbeat step up a couple of notches. However much he'd tried to reassure himself that failure to get onto the team wouldn't be the end of the world, in his soul he knew that was a lie.

I have to make it!

'We'll start with the 5,000 metres, work our way through the 1,500 metres and end up with the 800 metres,' said Brother Colm.

AK would be in this last group. Part of him felt pleased because he'd have a bit more preparation time, but part of him just wanted to get it over with and get a nod from Brother Colm.

As the 5,000-metre boys made their way to their starting places, AK walked over to Musa, stretching his arms and his legs as he walked.

'Going last, eh?' said Musa. 'That will give us time to find you a sponsor and some advertising partners.'

'In your dreams,' laughed AK.

'Nervous?'

'I just hope Fumo trips over a cockroach or develops a third leg.'

Fumo was arrogant, boastful and a legendary wind-up merchant. Unfortunately, he was also an extremely gifted 800-metre runner.

It was Musa's turn to laugh. 'You don't need to worry about Fumo. He's nowhere near your class!'

The 5,000- and 1,500-metre trials were a blur for AK, as he was pacing about trying to mentally and physically prepare himself for his own race. Finally Brother Colm called the 800-metre runners forward. AK was in the first heat.

'Good luck!' said Musa, giving AK a thumbs-up.

As AK walked over to Brother Colm with seven other 800-metre runners, Fumo fell into step with him. 'May the best man win,' grinned Fumo, 'which in this case is… me.'

AK tried to blot out the annoying twang of Fumo's voice but it was hard when he was standing less than a metre away.

'Right,' said Brother Colm, checking his clipboard and ticking off the boys' names. 'I know this is a big race for you but the key is to not let the pressure get to you. Be yourselves out there. Right?'

AK swallowed nervously and nodded with the others.

'Good,' smiled Brother Colm. 'Now, I want Abasi in Lane 1 and Daniel in Lane 2.'

Brother Colm proceeded to read out the names of the other runners and their allotted lanes. AK was given Lane 7, one lane away from the outside lane, which had been assigned to Fumo. He groaned. How could he run his best race with Fumo on his shoulder?

Fumo winked at AK as they reached their respective starting lines. AK stretched his arms high above his head and closed his eyes.

I am a runner. I have speed. I can beat the wind.

'It might be better to keep your eyes open during the race,' mocked Fumo, 'unless you specifically want to fall over!'

'Can you keep that mouth of yours closed for a few seconds!' hissed AK.

The 800 metres has a staggered start, as the outside runners initially have further to run than those on the inside lanes. So Fumo's starting line in Lane 8 was in front of everyone else's, with AK's a short distance behind him in Lane 7.

AK positioned himself on the Lane 7 white start line, left foot in front of right, fists clenched and ready. An older boy called Jamil checked everyone's start position to make sure no one was stepping beyond their white line and gaining an unfair advantage, and when he was satisfied that the runners were all standing correctly, he waved to Brother Colm.

AK waited for Brother Colm's starting orders, his body primed to move.

'Take your marks!' called Brother Colm. 'Get set!'

I'm going to win, mouthed Fumo.

'Go!'

AK sprang forward.

The race was on.

CHAPTER 3

THE RACE

AK got off to a good start, his feet hitting the track, his body moving fluidly. He had nearly caught Fumo by the first bend, when the runners broke and everyone made a dash for the inside lane.

During an 800-metre race, AK usually ran high up the field with one foot in Lane 1 and the other in Lane 2. He liked to maintain a position in the first three, and then kick off just after the last bend to go for first place.

When everyone broke, a boy called Othenio took pole position in Lane 1. AK made second – half-and-half in Lanes 1 and 2 – just behind Othenio's shoulder. Fumo took third in Lane 1, close behind AK. By the end of the first lap these first three positions were exactly the same, and AK took a quick look round. The rest of the pack was now a considerable distance behind the front three. The winner would be AK, Fumo or Othenio. Of that AK was certain.

AK was satisfied with his position, but he could sense Fumo right behind him, giving nothing away, and almost touching him. This was intensely irritating and AK would have liked to lash out and shove Fumo off the track, but he suspected Brother Colm wouldn't take too kindly to this.

As they entered the last two hundred metres, Othenio tried to pull away, but AK wasn't having it. Hc matched Othenio step for step, while Fumo kept right up there too.

As they approached the final bend AK made his move, tapping into the energy reserves he'd stored. In a few quick strides he passed Othenio. There were now just eighty metres to go and he was in the lead; the race was there for the taking.

At the fifty-metre mark he was still first and running at speed, but as he hit forty metres, he felt a presence in his slipstream and Fumo suddenly sprinted past him.

No!

AK accelerated but it was no good. With twenty metres to go, Fumo had a couple of metres on him and however hard AK pushed himself he simply couldn't reach him. A second later Fumo sped past the finish line, with AK in second.

AK knelt down on the track and put his head in his hands. He'd been beaten by his arch-rival. He hadn't made the team.

'You ran a good race,' crowed Fumo, patting AK on the shoulder. 'Just not good enough!'

While Fumo went off to celebrate with his friends, AK slowly staggered to his feet, the pain of defeat like a spear in his heart.

'Come on, AK, there's no need for drama!'

It was Brother Colm.

AK hung his head, feeling resignation and defeat coursing through his body. 'I'm sorry,' he mumbled.

'Don't be sorry!' Brother Colm smiled. 'You can't win every race. Even David Rudisha and Mo Farah experience their share of defeats.'

'I know, but at least they made their school athletics teams.'

'Who says you haven't made the team?' asked Brother Colm.

AK lifted his head in surprise.

'That's right. I've got room for two 800-metre specialists in your age category and I want you on the team.'

'Yes!' shouted AK, punching the air in delight.

'Look, AK,' said Brother Colm, 'I know you dream of being a running legend, and that's great. You're surrounded in Iten by role models and amazingly successful athletes. But a couple of the other teachers have told me that your attitude towards your work can be, how shall I put this, a little bit unenthusiastic, and that's something I worry about.'

AK abruptly stopped his celebrations. 'I'll try harder in class, Brother Colm, I promise.' He was afraid the coach might suddenly change his mind and push AK *off* the team.

'You do that,' said Brother Colm. 'Because for every runner who bags a gold medal, there are hundreds who don't make it. Do you get me?'

AK nodded earnestly.

'Excellent. Now off you go and I'll see you at the Athletics Team meet tomorrow after school.'

Yes! AK couldn't disguise his delight. Sure, Fumo had beaten him in this race but Brother Colm believed in him enough to put him on the team. AK would show Fumo what a truly great runner he was.

'Why are you smiling?' asked a confused-looking Musa, who was standing by the side of the track. 'You came second.'

'Brother Colm's taking Fumo *and* me on the team,' replied AK proudly.

'Nice one!' shouted Musa, his face breaking into a broad smile. 'We'll see if we can put a kit deal in place before the big event.'

They both laughed and high-fived, while Fumo looked over at them with a suspicious glare.

AK hurried into the building, got changed quickly and headed back to the track to meet up with Musa again. When he got there he was shocked to see Musa talking to AK's father.

A shudder of fear hit AK. Why on earth was his dad here? His family lived sixty miles away. Had something terrible happened to his mum, or his little sister Bibi?

He hurried over, anxiety pulsing through him.

'Dad? What's going on?'

'Hi, AK.' Dad smiled and put his arm round his son's shoulder.

'Is everything OK with Mum and Bibi?' demanded AK.

'They're fine.'

'So what's the emergency?'

'There's no emergency. I just need to talk to you.'

Musa, sensing it was time for a dad and lad moment, said he had to go and do some maths homework – a first for him – and disappeared inside the building.

'Let's walk,' said Dad.

They strolled over the grass leading away from the running track.

'What's this about?' asked AK, sure that Dad must have some pretty big news if he'd made the journey.

'You know my work in the lab?'

AK nodded. His dad was working on some big international science project – something to do with particles. Whenever Dad tried to talk to AK about the specifics of the project AK's eyes glazed over and he started feeling sleepy.

'Unfortunately something went seriously wrong with the project a few days ago and we've all been summoned to London to rectify the situation. The people running the project have acted incredibly quickly. They've already sorted out our flights and accommodation.'

'How long will you be gone?' asked AK.

'After we've sorted out this problem, the people running the project want us to stay in England for the next big stage, so that mistakes like this don't happen again. So we'll be there for about a year.'

'A year!' blurted out AK. 'You're leaving us for a whole year!'

'Not quite,' said Dad. 'You, Mum and Bibi are coming with me.'

AK felt as if he'd just been rammed in the solar plexus with a shaft of metal. 'What are you talking about? I'm not going to England. I've just made an athletics team led by the best running coach on earth!'

'I know it's a wrench,' said Dad softly, 'but St Patrick's have agreed to keep your place open. And although a year sounds like a long time, I'm sure it will fly by. Plus there's bound to be some top-class running coaches in London, and because we all speak excellent English we'll acclimatize very quickly.'

AK's mum had been born in England and lived there for the first eleven years of her life, so AK and Bibi had been brought up totally bilingual.

'I don't want another running coach!' shouted AK, looking at his father as if he was a grotesque beast who'd just descended from the heavens to smite him with a plague. 'I'm not coming!'

'I'm sorry, AK, but it's a Mum and Dad decision, and it's been made. You have to get your stuff together.'

'What do you mean?' asked AK, fighting back the tears.

'We need to go home now and get ready,' replied Dad. 'Our flight leaves tomorrow at midday.'

CHAPTER 4

THIS IS LONDON

AK had never been on a plane before. The flight to England should have been one of the most exciting journeys of his life but he was too stunned to enjoy a single second. He ate the two meals morosely, hardly looking at the food, and rebuffed any attempts by his family to start even the most simple conversation.

He'd pleaded with his father on the athletics track at St Patrick's to let him stay behind in Iten. He'd begged him before saying a tearful goodbye to Musa. ('As your best friend I'm devastated,' said Musa, smiling bravely, 'but as your business manager I see commercial opportunities in Europe.') And he'd argued with both his parents that night at home.

None of it had made any difference. Everything AK cherished and loved had been left behind in Kenya like a discarded sack of rubble. He hadn't even been able to find Brother Colm to say goodbye, so he'd just had to leave a hurriedly scrawled note.

'Come on, AK,' said Mum several times during the flight. 'It won't be that bad, I promise.'

But how could she know? If you wanted to be a top 800-metre runner, St Patrick's was the finest place on earth. With a whole year spent away from the school and Brother Colm, AK would fall behind Fumo and all of the others. His running career had just been effectively ended.

As they touched down at Heathrow Airport at 6pm local time, AK's spirits sunk even lower. A light drizzle ran down the plane's windows, and the second he stepped outside a freezing wind bit into his flesh. In spite of his parents' positive smiles he could see that they too were shocked by this harsh change of climate. The only one who seemed to be happy was Bibi, who ran over the tarmac trying to catch raindrops in her mouth.

After they had passed through passport control and collected their luggage, Mum led them towards a taxi rank and handed a driver a piece of paper with their new address.

'The guys running the project said this place would suit us perfectly,' Dad announced. AK scowled.

As the taxi sped down the motorway, AK took in the large expanses of dark green grass by the roadside, such a contrast with the browns and reds of Iten. After leaving the motorway they entered more built-up areas with buildings looming over the taxi like strange grey beasts. Shops and pubs and bus stops whizzed by, illuminated by a haze of pale yellow light.

'This is London,' said the driver as they passed a large railway station by the side of the road. Now there were far more cars about, and neon lights showering bursts of light onto the pavements and road.

An hour later the taxi stopped outside a two-storey red-brick Victorian house that was squeezed into the middle of a street crammed with identical-looking properties.

'This area's called Kentish Town,' explained the driver. 'There's an underground station round the corner and plenty of buses to get you around.'

'We have the whole house?' asked Bibi with a squeal of delight after they'd climbed out with their bags and the taxi had gone.

'We have the bottom part.' Mum reached for a key and twisted it in the lock. The door opened onto a small hallway with a flecked dark blue carpet. There were two further doors marked FLAT 1 and FLAT 2. Mum turned another key in the FLAT 1 door and they walked through.

They found themselves in a narrow corridor with three doors on the left-hand side. They cautiously tried each one in turn like archaeologists on a dig. The first led to a small white-tiled bathroom, the second to a decent-sized kitchen. Both Mum and Dad grinned excitedly when they saw the gleaming appliances.

'Talk about modern gadgets!' said Mum.

'What's the big deal about a washing machine?' grumbled AK.

The third door led to Mum and Dad's bedroom. This was much bigger than their bedroom back home and they both made admiring comments about the size of the bed, the light yellow wallpaper and the neat, wooden bedside tables.

At the end of the corridor were two further doors. One led to a good-sized sitting room with two beige sofas, a light brown armchair and a flat screen TV. Even though AK had instructed himself not to show satisfaction with anything he came across in London, he had to admit that the TV did look impressive.

The last room was AK and Bibi's bedroom. There was a small desk with an office chair, a tall white wardrobe, and curtains with funny black squiggles on a crimson background. The sleeping quarters were wooden bunk beds. AK said he didn't care where he slept because he didn't want to be there anyway, so Bibi plumped for the bottom bunk.

Mum went to the airing cupboard outside the bathroom to switch on the heating. 'This will warm us all up,' she said. 'Now, who wants to come to the shops and buy some food?'

'Me!' shouted Bibi.

'What about you, AK?' asked Mum.

'No,' said AK.

Mum pulled AK towards her but he evaded her attempt to hug him and went off to his bedroom. He dumped his bag on the floor and climbed up to the top bunk where he lay down and fumed silently.

A few minutes later Dad popped his head round the door. 'How's it going?'

'Just great!' said AK sourly. 'I'm stuck in a freezing city away from everything I love.'

Dad came into the room. 'You've got us three. That's good, isn't it?'

AK said nothing.

'I know it's a massive change,' said Dad sympathetically, 'but we'll all get used to it quicker than you think. Why don't I take you out for a run tomorrow?'

'No thanks.'

'Come on, mate,' said Dad. 'It's all going to be OK.'

'Correction,' said AK, propping himself up on his elbows. '*You'll* be OK because you've got your science mates. *Mum* will be OK because she'll be meeting the midwives at the hospital and *Bibi* will be OK because she makes millions of new friends wherever she goes.'

'And so will you be OK,' cut in Dad.

'No, I won't!' snapped AK. 'I'm going to hate everyone here. I know I am. I just want to be back with Musa at St Patrick's.'

'I know,' said Dad, 'but it's only a year. The time will fly by.'

'I don't think so,' AK hit back.

They were silent for a few moments and then Dad spoke again. 'The people running my project have already sorted out school places for everyone's kids – they did it in record time. They've got you signed up for the local school. It's called Barker Academy and apparently it's doing really well.'

In all of his bitterness and rage AK hadn't really considered what he'd do about school in England. Just the thought of it made his hands go clammy.

'And Barker Academy want you to start tomorrow morning,' said Dad.

AK sat bolt upright in shock. 'Tomorrow?' he cried.

Dad nodded.

This was unbelievable. How could his parents do this to him? First they moved him to a new country, now he was going to start a brand new school in… a few hours. Could his life possibly get any worse?

CHAPTER 5

FIRST DAY

The Barker Academy was a five-minute walk from the flat. From the outside it looked as if five giant white dice had been chucked into the air and glued together where they landed.

'Interesting-looking building,' said Dad, trying to sound upbeat.

'Looks like a dump,' muttered AK.

The woman behind the reception desk got Mum to fill out several forms. She then sold them the school's uniform – a pair of black trousers, a white shirt and a blue and black striped blazer. AK was instructed to go to the boys' toilet across the hallway, to change into his new uniform. The trousers and shirt were OK. The blazer was itchy and uncomfortable.

'You look great!' trilled Mum when he emerged and handed her his other clothes.

'Well done!' beamed the receptionist. 'I've phoned for someone to come and get you. Your parents and sister are free to go now.'

Mum, Dad and Bibi took turns hugging AK, which was very embarrassing.

'Good luck!' Dad grinned. Then the three of them made their way towards the exit. A few seconds later they were gone and AK suddenly felt anxious and alone.

A girl AK's age, with long dark hair and large brown eyes, appeared through a blue door.

'You must be AK.' She walked over to him with a smile. 'I'm Perminder. You're in my form. I'll take you up to meet everyone.'

AK's body tingled with nerves as he followed her through the blue door. They climbed two flights of stairs, entered a corridor and took the second door on the right.

A group of about twenty-five students were sitting at tables in a whitewashed classroom listening to a man in a brown suit, with a goatee beard and intense green eyes.

'There you are!' said the man standing up and shaking AK's hand. 'Welcome to Barker's, it's a pleasure to meet you. I'm Mr Sells, your form teacher. Guys, this is AK. He joins us at very short notice from Kenya. From the brief information we've been sent, AK...' Mr Sells studied a sheet of paper. 'I see you're a very fine runner from a school with an unbelievable athletics record.'

'I'm OK,' blushed AK.

'What's your distance?'

'800 metres.'

'Well, I'm sure Miss Jenkins will want to make your acquaintance pretty sharpish.' Mr Sells grinned. 'She's our head of PE and she's just a tiny bit competitive!'

There was laughter round the room.

'Why don't you sit next to Perminder?' suggested Mr Sells.

AK followed Perminder to a table at the back. They passed a girl with short bleached blonde hair and a tattoo on her left hand. She waved at them. Perminder waved back.

'I want everyone to make AK feel as welcome as possible,' said Mr Sells. 'Imagine what it would be like for you to leave your home country and go somewhere totally new.'

'I'd move to Hollywood and be a film star!' called out a boy with short spiked hair and very red cheeks. Several people laughed.

'OK,' said Mr Sells. 'Period One starts in a couple of minutes. Nice to meet you, AK, please feel free to come and see me if there are any problems at all. Good luck with your first day!'

AK nodded his thanks and then it was time for his first lesson.

Unfortunately it was maths, but he was relieved to discover that he was quite a bit ahead of what the class was doing. It was a double lesson, followed by break.

Perminder walked with AK out to the playground. All around them were noise and activity. Some kids were playing football, others were play-fighting and lots were just standing around talking.

'So what do you think of Barker Academy so far?' asked Perminder.

'It seems OK,' replied AK, 'but it's very different from my school back home.'

'I'm sure you'll get used to it soon,' smiled Perminder. 'The rest of us have!'

At that moment they were joined by the girl with blonde hair.

'This is Kathy,' said Perminder. 'When we're not arguing, we're best mates.'

'I'm *always* her best mate,' Kathy said with a grin. 'It's just that she get a bit moody sometimes. Watch you don't get on the wrong side of her!'

'Moody yourself!' Perminder hit back. 'Anyway, we'd better tell you about the teachers, AK. You know, the psychos, the nutters, the killers.'

'That just about covers all of them,' said Kathy.

AK grinned.

'Mr Sells thinks he's down with the kids, you know, very street, very cool, but he's all right really,' said Perminder.

'The one you have to watch out for is Miss Clarke,' said Kathy. 'She was born without a sense of humour, and when she loses it you're stuffed!'

AK listened to their banter and laughed, his brain trying to process everything. He'd just moved from an all-boys school in the sunniest setting in the world to a mixed school in a grey and barren wasteland, and now he was hanging out with two wisecracking girls. It was completely surreal.

Perminder and Kathy continued the teacher briefing after their art class, and kept it up well into lunch break in the canteen.

The canteen was a cavernous space with a serving hatch at one end and space for about five hundred kids at grey trestle tables. Everywhere the clank of cutlery and the sound of boisterous chatter filled the air.

Perminder and Kathy were two of the world's fastest talkers but they seemed genuinely interested in AK's life back home in Kenya. When prompted he told them about Musa and St Patrick's, and a little about his running ambitions. After lunch was over, they all had English with Mrs Robson, who turned out to be very pleasant, and told AK about a friend of hers who'd lived in Nairobi.

When the bell went for the end of school, AK was stunned to realize he'd actually enjoyed the day. For some unfathomable reason, Perminder and Kathy had adopted him, and their chatter and jokes had made everything go pretty quickly. They weren't Musa, but they could make him laugh.

'Shall we walk you home?' asked Kathy as she and Perminder grabbed their bags from their lockers.

'I'm going to see if I can find Miss Jenkins,' replied AK. 'You know, ask about the athletics set-up here.'

'Cool,' said Perminder. 'Get your running shoes on and we'll turn out for you when you make it to the Olympics.'

AK found Miss Jenkins in a small office on the far side of the building. The door was open. There were posters of famous sportspeople on the walls along with memos and letters and reminders on yellow Post-it notes. Miss Jenkins was just finishing a phone call. She held up a finger to tell AK she'd only be a minute.

Miss Jenkins was young and wiry, with thin lips, freckles on her left cheek and brown hair that was scraped into a tight ponytail. She was wearing a white and turquoise tracksuit and white trainers.

'Er, hi,' said AK when she'd finished her call. 'I'm AK. I've just got here from Kenya.'

'Ah, yes. Mr Sells mentioned you at lunch time – the famous runner from Iten! There was a big article in the *Sunday Times* about your school a few weeks ago. Is it Brother Colin who's the running man?'

'Brother Colm,' AK corrected her, impressed that she'd heard of him. 'I just wanted to say hello and see what's happening with the running side of things over here.'

'At the moment my time is totally taken up with the boys' and girls' football teams,' sighed Miss Jenkins. 'We've got some big tournaments coming up. Give me a couple of weeks and we'll get you out on the track, put you through your paces.'

Two weeks! AK was stunned.

'There's a running club over in Camden but they're not taking any new members at the moment,' added Miss Jenkins. 'The Fenton Harriers are supposed to be good but they're about ten miles away and it's a nightmare to get there. I could phone them if you like.'

'Nah,' said AK, 'it's fine.'

He left Miss Jenkins' office in a daze. Wait two weeks or go on a nightmare journey when all he had to do at St Patrick's was step outside? No thanks!

AK's enjoyment of his first day was suddenly mowed down by a feeling of shock and dejection. He wouldn't be able to run here. Maybe his athletics days really *were* over.

CHAPTER 6

TINNISON

'How was school?' asked Mum when AK walked in ten minutes later.

'Terrible.'

'Oh.' Mum's face fell.

'My school is amazing!' beamed Bibi, running up to AK. 'My teacher is called Miss Grant and she made me star of the day on my first day – can you believe it? And there's this amazing climbing equipment in the playground!'

'That's great.' AK managed a weak smile.

'And Dad's bringing home pizza for supper!'

AK liked pizza but a takeaway wasn't exactly going to cheer him up about lack of running opportunities at school, so he shrugged his shoulders and went to his bedroom. Mrs Robson had handed him a copy of their current English set text – *1984* by George Orwell. It was pretty heavy-duty stuff, set in a future society where no citizen is ever free from the eye of the omnipresent Big Brother, but the story was gripping and before he knew it he'd read forty pages.

'I'm home!' called out Dad a while later.

AK checked his watch. It was just after 6.30. He shuffled into the corridor. Dad stood there, briefcase in one hand, two cardboard pizza boxes in the other.

'How did things go at school?' asked Dad.

'In comparison to St Patrick's? Appalling.'

'It will get better,' said Dad.

If AK heard another positive statement from either of his parents, he'd scream.

The pizza was good – even AK had to admit that – but he stuck to his non-talkative mode to make sure his parents knew the depths of unhappiness they had caused him.

***

The following morning was even colder than the day before and AK shivered as he got dressed. He would never, repeat never, get used to living in a climate like this. He was amazed that people weren't dropping dead all over the place from hypothermia.

When he reached the end of his street and turned the corner for the Barker Academy road, he spotted the spiky-haired boy from his form – the one who'd cracked the Hollywood film star joke yesterday. He was standing arguing with a large man with greasy hair and a hooded green sweatshirt. They were shouting and although AK couldn't hear what they were saying, it didn't look particularly pleasant.

The boy suddenly turned to face AK. 'What are you looking at?' he demanded, striding angrily towards him.

'Nothing,' replied AK.

'Just because you fancy yourself as a runner doesn't mean you can spy on other people's business!' snarled the boy. 'I'm having a private conversation with my dad. So get lost!'

'I wasn't spying on you!' protested AK.

'Have you got some kind of problem?' demanded the boy.

'Leave the kid alone,' said the grubby man, but the boy lunged forward and gave AK a hard shove in the

chest. AK flew backwards and just managed to stop
himself crashing onto the floor.

'Leave him alone, Tinnison!' yelled a harsh voice.
It was Kathy. She had appeared at AK's side with
Perminder right behind her, and was glaring furiously
at his attacker.

'This is nothing to do with you!' spat out the boy.

'You're pathetic!' snapped Kathy. 'Come on, AK,
let's go.'

As they walked off, the boy and his dad started
shouting at each other again.

'Are you OK?' asked Perminder when they were a decent distance away.

'Yeah.' AK shuddered slightly. It didn't exactly feel good to be set upon on your second morning in a new country, only to be rescued by a girl, albeit clearly a tough one.

'That idiot's called Ray Tinnison,' Kathy said. 'His dad's a mess up, and his mum left them ages ago. Ray tends to take out his anger on whoever happens to be around. It's best to steer clear of him.'

'Thanks for stepping in,' said AK gratefully.

'No problem!' Kathy laughed. 'There's nothing like exchanging verbals with Ray Tinnison before school. Come on, we need to hurry. I can't be late again or I'll be for the chop!'

***

AK saw Ray Tinnison in the corridor that morning but Ray was speaking to someone on his mobile and didn't even notice AK. Luckily they didn't have any lessons together that morning and AK was pleased to have Perminder and Kathy with him in French and geography. Perminder said that Ray and his father were morons and losers. But AK still felt uneasy. At

St Patrick's there was a lot of joking around but no one had pushed him like Ray had done this morning. He must be pretty angry to pick on AK just because he thought AK was *looking* at him.

In the canteen at lunchtime AK sat with the girls, keeping an eye on the people around their table.

'If it's Ray Tinnison you're worried about, forget it,' said Kathy. 'If he touches you again, I'll punch his lights out.'

'Yeah,' said Perminder. 'There's three of us and only one of him. We could easily take him down!'

AK smiled weakly.

The rest of the day was fine, until the last lesson – PE.

AK was disturbed to discover that Ray Tinnison was in his PE group. Miss Jenkins took the lesson. It was football in the school gym. The place stank of stale sweat and chemical cleaning products. At the far end some older pupils were shooting baskets and laughing among themselves.

Although AK's primary sporting love was running, he also enjoyed playing and watching football. He hadn't tried out for the St Patrick's football team, but he was a decent player.

His stamina and running ability were useful for playing on the wing.

AK and Ray were on opposing teams and as soon as Miss Jenkins blew the whistle AK knew that Ray was going to be on his case. Ray made sure he played on the right so that he could face AK who was playing left wing. The first tackle was a little rash, the second was the type that could break someone's leg. AK just managed to leap out of the way at the last second. Someone was blocking Miss Jenkins' view so she didn't see it.

AK moved to the centre of the pitch to get away from Ray but in the last minute of the game, Ray slid in and caught AK on the side of his right foot. AK fell onto the ground clutching his ankle.

Miss Jenkins blew her whistle furiously. 'Ray, what are you playing at?' she shouted.

'I played the ball, Miss!' he protested, his face red with fury.

'Are you alright, AK?' asked Miss Jenkins, hurrying over to him and crouching on the floor.

'I'm fine.' AK got to his feet and hobbled over to the side of the pitch. He was worried that Ray had done some serious damage to his ankle, but after a few tentative steps and a light jog, AK was satisfied his ankle was bruised but nothing worse.

Miss Jenkins blew her whistle for the game to end and the players trooped off the pitch.

'Not such a big shot now, are you, Mr Olympic Runner?' hissed Ray on the way back to the changing room.

AK thought about finding Kathy and Perminder and telling them what had happened in the PE lesson but he decided this would be acting like a telltale little kid, and besides, it would probably lead to more trouble. No, for the time being he'd deal with Ray Tinnison by himself.

CHAPTER 7

RUNNING ROUND IN CIRCLES

For the next few days, AK was even quieter and less communicative at home. The Ray Tinnison incidents were bothering him, as was the school's running set-up, or rather, lack of one. He heard Mum and Dad whispering, and was sure they were talking about him, but he didn't care. He'd told them how bad things were going to be for him in London and he'd been proved right.

At school he still hung out with Kathy and Perminder but spoke little. Whenever they asked him if he was OK, he said he was just tired. And as for the lack of sunshine…

On Saturday morning the doorbell rang. AK was lying on his bunk flicking through an old running magazine he'd brought with him. It had an article about David Rudisha's training programme; he must have read it about a hundred times.

'Is AK in?' he heard a familiar voice ask, when Mum opened the flat door.

'Sure,' said Mum brightly. 'Who shall I say is calling?'

'I'm Perminder and this is Kathy. We're mates of his from school.'

'Would you like to come in?' asked Mum, but by this time, AK was out of his room and by the front door, embarrassment flooding through him.

'Want to come out for a bit?' asked Kathy.

'OK.' AK grabbed his coat.

'Fancy not telling me about your new friends!' said AK's mother, putting on a mock-scolding voice.

'Mum!' groaned AK, hurrying outside.

He wasn't sure where Perminder and Kathy were intending to go. It turned out that their minds were on window-shopping for clothes, an experience that bored AK to tears. He waited by changing rooms as the girls picked out jackets and coats they were never going to buy. But they made up for it by taking him to a café and buying him a Coke and a plate of teacakes, which tasted delicious.

'So what about your running then?' asked Kathy, stirring a fifth sugar into her tea. 'Been doing much?'

'No,' replied AK, taking a sip of Coke. 'Miss Jenkins is too busy and the nearest running club is miles away.'

'That sounds a bit rubbish,' said Perminder. 'Were the facilities back home much better?'

AK gave them a quick introduction to Iten and its remarkable running history.

'Wow,' said Kathy. 'That Brother Colm guy sounds like a total genius!'

'Yep, he's the best. There are probably more running champions living in Iten than anywhere else in the world.'

They were silent for a few minutes and then Perminder spoke. 'Just because you haven't got a coach doesn't mean you can't run. I saw a TV show about swimmers a few weeks ago and loads of them practise by themselves.'

'I know,' nodded AK, 'but there's so much technique and strategy involved in my race – the 800

57

metres. I need someone experienced to help me out, to improve me. Without that I'll never make it.'

'Well, I think Perminder's right,' said Kathy, wiping her lips on the back of a napkin. 'Start by yourself and sooner or later you'll find someone.'

The conversation changed to the most outrageous punishments Miss Clarke had ever given, and Kathy's tale of a three-hour after-school detention seemed to top the others.

When AK said goodbye to Perminder and Kathy an hour later and started the walk home, he went over what they'd both said.

Just because you haven't got a coach doesn't mean you can't run.

Start by yourself and sooner or later you'll find someone.

He thought about it for the rest of the day.

***

Just after 10am on Sunday morning, he made a decision. He grabbed his trainers from his cupboard and changed into his running gear. He found his parents in the kitchen.

'Hey, AK,' beamed Dad. 'It's good to see you in

your kit again!'

'Are you going running with those two girls?' asked Mum.

'No,' replied AK. 'Apparently there's a park somewhere near here. I'm just going to do some laps.'

'Great idea!' said Dad. 'Do you want me to come with you?'

'Nah, I'll be fine.'

He'd heard there was a park about half a mile away and after asking a couple of people for instructions he found it. It wasn't an enormous space but it had a decent sized bed of grass at its centre, with an oval path encircling it that provided a circuit of about two hundred metres. There were a few bushes and a couple of trees on the park's perimeter. Around the edges of the park were wooden benches. Three of these were currently occupied by a young couple with a baby, someone in a hoodie reading the paper, and an elderly woman feeding some pigeons.

AK did some stretches, shivering in the icy climate and wondering how his body would adapt to running in conditions like this. He jogged to the fence and back a couple of times and then did some more stretches. He looked at the tarmac path. Four laps of the two-hundred-metre circuit would give him eight hundred metres.

He did his first 800, feeling the blood pounding round his body and the sharp wind on his face. It felt good, despite the cold. He did a second 800 and then a third.

Rudisha had run 1:40:91 at the London Olympics and AK had set his sights on achieving 1:50 by the end of the year. His current personal best was 1:52:28, timed by Brother Colm on the athletics track at St Patrick's. How AK was going to achieve this without a coach or any running partners was beyond him, but if he didn't start training again now, he'd have no chance whatsoever.

He did a fourth and fifth 800 metres and started to feel the nerve endings and muscles really kicking into life. Maybe he could continue his running in England. Sure, he had no coach at present, but wasn't self-motivation something that Brother Colm always encouraged?

***

On Monday he was in a much better mood at school,

less worried about Ray Tinnison and pleased that he'd been for his first run in London. He went straight to the park at the end of the day. Once again, he warmed up, jogged, did some sprints and ended with four goes at the 800 metres. The guy in the hoodie was there again, siting hunched on one of the park benches. There was also a group of older girls, laughing raucously and a man reading an incredibly thick chemistry textbook.

On Tuesday AK went to the park for a third time. The guy in the hoodie was the only other person there. AK did some stretches and jogs and was about to start some sprints when the guy in the hoodie stood up and started walking across the park in AK's direction. When he was halfway across he dropped his hood and AK was amazed to see Ray Tinnison's dad.

He was walking directly towards AK. 'Can I have a word?' he called out.

AK looked behind him, but there was no one there. This led to one conclusion. Ray Tinnison's dad wanted to talk to him. And he was now just five metres away.

CHAPTER 6

AN UNEXPECTED OFFER

Mr Tinnison didn't look like he was in great shape. His face was covered in stubble, his clothes looked like they hadn't been washed for weeks, and his boots were encrusted with mud.

'I saw you with my son, Ray, the other day, didn't I?' said Mr Tinnison.

AK nodded slowly.

'Ray mentioned you're from Kenya, is that right? He said you're a bit of a runner. I've been watching you for the last few days in this park.'

A bolt of fear stabbed at AK's insides. Was the man a psycho who had been staking him out? He looked around the empty park and eyed Ray's dad suspiciously. If he made any sinister moves, AK would be out of there in a nanosecond.

'My name's Frank,' said Ray's dad. His face was pockmarked – the remains of what must have been vicious teenage acne. 'I actually have a keen interest in running. At least, I used to…'

His sentence trailed off into the air and he fumbled in his coat pocket, pulled out a yellowing newspaper cutting and handed it over to AK. It was a very old article about an up-and-coming sixteen-year-old runner, with an accompanying black and white photo of a boy in running gear, crossing a finish line, with the rest of the race runners far behind.

'That was me,' said Frank. 'I'm the boy in the photo. I wanted to be a runner, wanted it really badly. I won some junior championships back in the day. They said I was destined for great things, but then I broke my leg in a motorbike accident just after my eighteenth birthday and my running career was over. Gone. I did some coaching badges but… well, things haven't quite gone the way I planned since then.'

AK looked from Frank's face to the youthful runner in the paper. It was impossible to tell if they were the same person. He handed the clipping back and Frank stuffed it into his coat pocket. Was this the right time to tell Frank that his son had nearly shattered AK's ankle in a PE lesson?

'I was working in a wood factory for a few months earlier this year, but the company went under and I lost my job.' Frank looked despondent. 'I know it's tough for everyone at the minute but there are times when I think someone's got it in for me. I spend most of my days moping on one of the benches here or sitting in front of mindless rubbish on the TV at home.'

There was silence for a few moments. AK had no idea what to say to all that. A stranger had just told him his whole life story. He was poised to make a dash for it if need be.

'Anyway,' Frank went on, 'that's enough about me and my troubles. The reason I wanted to talk to you is – I'm assuming that if you've just got to England, you haven't sorted out a coach yet, is that right?'

AK nodded slowly.

'So I was wondering if… well, if you'd like me to help you out with your running? Nothing flash, just some pointers. I never completed my coaching badges but I've been around a long time and know a

thing or two about how to improve a runner's ability.
I've never lost my interest in that.'

'You're… you're offering to coach me?' AK was
astonished. Frank didn't look in good enough shape
to walk to the underground station, let alone help AK
with his running. But AK's parents had always told
him not to judge a person by their appearance. Mind
you, he was pretty sure they wouldn't be too happy

about him hanging out with someone who looked like Frank.

'What do you say?' asked Frank. 'Just a bit of putting you through your paces. Getting you used to the climate over here. That kind of thing.'

AK frowned.

'If you don't want me to help you, that's absolutely fine,' added Frank. 'I know I look like a wreck. But it's something I'd be really keen on doing. And if you *are* good, I reckon I could make you better. Maybe we could both get something out of it.'

'I don't know,' said AK.

'Fine. The ball is totally in your court. But I'll be here at four tomorrow afternoon and I'd be very pleased if you showed up.'

'What about Ray?' asked AK anxiously. 'I'm sure he won't be too happy with you helping me out. We, er, haven't been getting on in school.'

'This is nothing to do with him. He doesn't need to know about it.' And with that, Frank nodded a goodbye and wandered out of the park.

The cogs in AK's mind whirred and clicked. Was Frank for real? Shouldn't he just wait for Miss Jenkins? After all, she was the school's PE leader and she was a qualified teacher. He'd be able to trust her. But then again, Miss Jenkins seemed really busy, and even if she did eventually put him through his paces, she wasn't a specialist running coach.

And if the newspaper clipping was real, if Frank was the young man in that photo, then he'd obviously been a decent runner. If he *had* smashed his leg in an accident then that wasn't his fault, was it? It sounded like he'd a few bad breaks, things like losing his job.

On the other hand, what if Frank was a psycho and this was just a ploy to kill AK? Mind you, they'd be meeting in this park – a very open and public space. It would be pretty hard to kill a teenager in broad daylight and get away with it. And AK was sure he could outrun the guy if he needed to.

AK stayed in the park for half an hour and did another series of laps before heading home. When he arrived there was much excitement in the living room. Dad had brought back a computer and had set up a Wi-Fi connection. AK grabbed the mouse and immediately emailed Musa, telling him a bit about his life in London, without mentioning the fact that the only friends he'd made so far were girls, and that Brother Colm might be replaced by a man in a filthy green hoodie who spent most of his days sitting around on park benches. AK told Musa how much he missed him and his life back in Iten.

Later, after Bibi had enjoyed a good go on her favourite virtual farming game, AK was delighted to receive an email from Musa, saying how life was nowhere near as good at St Patrick's without AK, and that Musa was hoping to name a new stadium after his running pal if he ever got planning permission... and several million dollars.

On Wednesday in school, AK was totally preoccupied with Frank Tinnison's offer. Should he go to the park today, or shouldn't he? If he didn't go, would he be missing an opportunity? If he did go, was he walking into a trap? Perminder knocked on his skull during lunch break and asked if anyone was in there, but AK was too engrossed with his thoughts to respond to the joke.

By home time he'd made up his mind. He was going to accept Frank's offer with one caveat: at the first sign of any weirdness, he'd be out of there like a speeding bullet train.

CHAPTER 9

IN TRAINING

Directly after school AK changed into his running gear, stuffed his school uniform in his rucksack and headed with trepidation to the park. He was fairly sure that Frank wouldn't be there.

But he was wrong.

'All right?' Frank was waiting by the gate. He was wearing the same grimy clothes and his hair was still a greasy mess; it wasn't exactly the look of a top-class coach.

'How are we going to work this?' asked AK, looking at Frank for any signs of weird behaviour or weapons.

'Well,' said Frank, as they stepped into the park, 'it would be good to do a few warm ups and then see your running style. After that we could do some timed laps. I reckon a circuit of the park is about a couple of hundred metres.'

AK nodded. That seemed like a reasonable plan and not the ramblings of a madman.

'Right,' said Frank, 'let's get cracking.'

AK did some stretches and light jogging, while Frank watched from the sidelines. He then ran a few laps under Frank's watchful eye. A couple of times he had to avoid dog-walkers or kids on scooters but this didn't really bother him.

'Your style is good,' said Frank when they met up again by the side of the path. 'At a couple of points you were a little bit too upright for my liking. That's fine for Michael Johnson, but your body shape is very different from his. It's just something to watch. Run fully upright and you'll lose several tenths of a second.'

AK nodded. He hadn't been aware of these lapses, but if it was true it was right for Frank to pick up on them.

'I was more of a 1,500-metres man myself,' said Frank, 'but I'm a keen student of the 800 metres. It's probably the most tactical of races. Look at Rudisha, Abubaker or even our own lad, Steve Cram, from all those years ago. They're all master tacticians, always going for the best position and the optimum break.'

'Rudisha's one of my heroes,' said AK.

'He's a good hero to have. Now let's work on your starts. If we make progress there, we'll move on to building up some stamina. How about that?'

'Sounds OK.'

They went to the furthest part of the path and Frank drew a line on the tarmac with a muddy branch. 'It's not exactly the Commonwealth Games,' he said, 'but it will suit our purposes.'

For the next half hour, AK repeatedly did starts and then ran for twenty metres. Frank stood in front of him, to his left, to his right and behind him. He offered a couple of tips about body position and stride length – similar to stuff that AK had done back home.

They stopped at 5.15.

'Well, I thought that was a decent start,' said Frank.

'It was all right,' said AK.

'So what do you reckon?' asked Frank hopefully. 'Do I qualify for the job? Will you be here same time tomorrow?'

AK mulled this question for a few moments. 'I'll see.'

'Fair enough.'

AK couldn't help but notice the dirt under Frank's fingernails and he questioned himself once again about working with someone who looked so unkempt and spent most of his time sitting around doing nothing.

'Maybe see you tomorrow then,' said Frank, before turning and walking towards the park's gates.

***

'You're back a bit late,' said Mum when AK got home.

'I've been doing some running training with… with… er, with Mr Tinnison.'

'Is he the school athletics coach?' asked Mum.

'Yeah, something like that. What's for supper?'

'I've done some fish and rice but you'll have to heat it up and serve it for you and Bibi, because I've got my first shift at the hospital and Dad won't be home till after nine.'

'No problem,' nodded AK, taking a carton of orange juice from the fridge and pouring himself a glass.

While Bibi snored softly in her bed that night, AK

lay on the top bunk and replayed the events of the afternoon. He'd seen enough of Frank to realize he knew some running stuff. That would never substitute for Brother Colm's amazing regime in Iten, but then again, Brother Colm wasn't here and, as Mum often said, sometimes you have to make do with the hand you're dealt.

***

AK met up with Frank on Thursday and Friday and they went through most of the stuff they'd done during their first session together. Frank then got AK to do some circuits, jumping up and down off park benches, doing press ups and running to the fence and back.

Saturday was a quiet day in AK's house. He watched TV, exchanged emails with Musa and thought about his new running regime.

On Sunday the whole family went to the Science Museum in South Kensington. Bibi was so excited by all of the interactive exhibits that she was like a moth fluttering at speed round a lamp. AK enjoyed the 3D exhibition and laughed at Bibi's manic enthusiasm.

On Monday, AK met up with Frank again. Frank adjusted AK's start position so that his body arced a fraction more forward. Frank said he'd been reading up on 800-metre strategies and had some new tips to pass on.

The next day they did a lot of work on stamina. Frank got AK to run six laps, and then seven and eight, before instructing him to start sprinting. There was a lot of legwork but AK felt it was worthwhile.

On Wednesday and Thursday they focused on the break after the first bend and this time, even though he was totally unfit, Frank ran a bit with AK, to give him a sense of another runner in his space.

'That nearly killed me!' panted Frank when they'd finished.

'You did OK,' said AK.

Although the cold weather wasn't pleasant, AK could feel his fitness levels building up again. He wondered what Brother Colm would say about his new running coach. Would he warn AK to break all ties with him or would he be encouraging?

After school on Friday Perminder and Kathy tried to get AK to come to the shops with them again, but he said he had other plans.

'Are you starting to run?' asked Kathy.

'Maybe I am, maybe I'm not.'

'Mr Mystery!' laughed Perminder.

That afternoon's session in the park was particularly good and it dawned on AK that he had started to trust Frank. He wasn't a nutcase or a murderer – he had a genuine interest in running. And he had some good ideas.

75

Frank pushed AK hard that afternoon. AK did fifty laps of the track and was completely exhausted by the end of it. But his body was bathed in the warm glow that surrounds you when you make use of so many muscles, and for the first time since he'd arrived in England he was in a good mood at home that evening. He was sure his parents noticed this change but they said nothing. Maybe they were worried that if they said anything about his upturned spirits, these spirits would melt away like a cloud of fog.

AK even read Bibi a bedtime story.

He spent Saturday afternoon with Perminder and Kathy at Perminder's flat, playing on her Xbox, listening to music and making endless rounds of toast. Although he had promised himself he wouldn't tell them about Frank, it just kind of slipped out.

'Ray Tinnison's father is coaching you?' gasped Kathy.

'Are you mad?' demanded Perminder.

'He actually knows a lot about athletics,' explained AK. 'He used to be a good runner himself. '

'But he's a total waste of space,' said Kathy. 'My mum sees him sitting on a park bench in the day, looking miserable and doing nothing.'

'I know, he's had some hard knocks and feels like bad luck has stalked him. But I've done a few days training with him and it's been really helpful.'

The girls looked at him as if he'd just sprouted purple wings.

'What does Ray have to say about this?' asked Perminder.

'He doesn't know.'

'Please, AK,' said Kathy. 'I think you're making a big mistake. Ray's dad might be dangerous. You know that desperate people do desperate things.'

'He's not dangerous,' replied AK firmly, 'and he's not desperate. There's a part of him that wants to be active – to do things. He's had a lot of problems. That doesn't make him a bad person.'

'Suit yourself,' said Perminder, 'but don't say we didn't warn you.'

AK was grateful for their concern but he was sure they were wrong. There was nothing sinister about Frank. He was OK.

On Sunday AK Skyped Musa, did some homework and took Bibi to see some crummy Disney film. It wasn't the greatest day of his life but nor was it the worst and his mood was certainly higher than a week ago. Running in the park and going over tactics with Frank had given him something to focus on.

Maybe living in England isn't going to be as bad as I first thought, he decided as he drifted off to sleep that night.

CHAPTER 10

A CHANCE TO RUN

The next two weeks passed incredibly quickly. Ray Tinnison barged past AK a couple of times in the school corridors but there was no repeat of the pushing incident or the violent football tackles.

At school he hung out with Perminder and Kathy. After school he met up with Frank. They worked on every aspect of running from diet and pre-race warm ups to head dipping at the finish line. AK got more and more used to running in cold weather, sometimes with a harsh wind propelling him forward or holding him back. AK was pleased that Frank was pushing him and looking for even the tiniest ways to improve his power and speed. And Frank started to open up a little bit about his own running days.

'The day I broke my leg was the worst day of my life,' Frank confessed during one of the short breaks they took during training. They were sitting on one of the benches. 'I had been so focused on running that I'd let everything else go: my family, my friends, my school work. After the crash it was like my life had been frozen at that point. It was incredibly hard to get over it. In fact, I don't think I've ever really got over it.'

AK looked at Frank's pained expression and thought about how terrible it must have been. There he was, poised for excellence on the running track, and the next minute his dream had been shattered to pieces.

It suddenly became clear to AK how Frank had managed to spiral so far downwards. It also made him think for the first time that maybe Brother Colm and his parents' insistence that he keep up with his studies might just be right.

In turn, AK told Frank about Brother Colm and St Patrick's. Frank was fascinated by all of the stuff about Brother Colm and spent some time looking him up on Google and marvelling at his incredible track record.

On the following Monday afternoon when AK got to the park, Frank dropped an incendiary device.

'I have some news,' he informed AK.

'What kind of news?'

'Yesterday I phoned up a mate from my running days. He's called Mike Rivers and he's very involved in youth athletics. He told me there's a big youth race meeting coming up at a place called the Finn Arena.'

'What's that got to do with me?'

'One of the races is the 800 metres,' said Frank. 'Mike mentioned that one of the boys pulled out last Thursday night. He's been looking for a suitable replacement but he hasn't found one yet. When I mentioned you he seemed really keen.'

'You're not serious?' blurted out AK.

'I am totally serious,' said Frank.

'But we've only been training for a few weeks!'

'I know, but what about all of the amazing coaching you've had back home? From the little I've seen of you, you have the potential to be a fine runner one day.'

'So you entered me for the race?' asked AK.

'No,' replied Frank, '*you* make that decision. I'm just saying there's a place up for grabs if you want it. If you say yes I have to phone Mike back tonight so he doesn't give the spot to someone else. What do you say?'

'Isn't it too early for me to be running races in England? Shouldn't I get a bit more acclimatized with the weather and things like that?'

'You could, but ultimately you need as much race experience as possible. If you don't want to do it, though, I totally understand.'

'When is it?' asked AK.

'Saturday.'

'*This* Saturday?' exploded AK. 'Are you joking?'

'No,' replied Frank. 'The event will run from 1pm to 5pm and your race will be very early on.'

AK bit his bottom lip. He should probably say no, carry on training for a few more weeks and then reconsider.

But on the other hand what did he have to lose? No one knew him in England. If he came last, no one would remember him. If he won, well, you never knew what might happen. Like Frank, Brother Colm was always very keen on 'seizing the day'.

'OK,' said AK. 'I'll do it, but it means we only have five days to prepare.'

'Good decision.' Frank smiled. 'I'll phone Mike later. Let's focus on your running now, beginning with stretches and warm-ups.

Following these they went over starts again and then Frank twice timed AK doing four laps of the oval path.

'Although your times are obviously affected by the quality of this track and the fact that there are people walking dogs and riding skateboards here, you're putting in some decent runs,' said Frank. 'That bodes well for Saturday. The track at the Finn Arena is supposed to be top notch.'

After this, AK did some sit-ups and push-ups, then some leg and calf stretches lying on the ground with his feet resting on one of the wooden park benches. Frank then ran a couple of laps with AK, Frank taking first place with AK running on his shoulder. When AK tried to break, Frank kept getting in his way and blocking him, so AK had to move sidewards and gain more space. Each time, with a bit of grit and determination, AK managed to overtake Frank.

'You should save the sprint finish for the last hundred metres, ideally somewhere between ninety and sixty,' said Frank when they took a quick break. 'If you go too early you'll run out of juice.'

Their session lasted almost two hours, and once they had finished they sat on a bench talking about Saturday's race. A couple of sparrows landed on a tree branch above them, and a smart-suited man hurried past.

'What happens if I totally humiliate myself?' asked AK.

'That's far more likely to happen to me.' Frank smiled.

'But you'll be on the sidelines,' pointed out AK. 'I'll be out there on the track for everyone to see.'

'You've got nothing to worry about. This is your first race over here. It's a great chance to get a real feel for running competitively in this country.'

***

AK said nothing to his parents about Saturday's race. He didn't want them meeting Frank Tinnison. He didn't want them seeing Frank's scuffed jeans and tatty hoodie. He also didn't want to admit that he'd been lying to them all along when he'd told them that Frank was a sports teacher at school.

On Tuesday in school AK made himself concentrate. He couldn't afford to be held back at the end of the day for not keeping up with his work. He had a major race to run on Saturday and he needed all of the training time possible.

Frank was there at 4pm, and immediately told him that Mike Rivers had confirmed his place in Saturday's 800-metre race.

They were just about to start their day's session when a figure burst into the park, flinging the iron gates open with a loud clang.

AK looked round and saw the agitated figure of Ray Tinnison storming over towards them. Frank seemed just as shocked as AK. He opened his mouth to speak, but Ray got in there first.

'What the hell is going on?' he roared.

CHAPTER 11

FATHER AND SON

'alm down!' said Frank. 'Nothing's going on.'

'I overheard Perminder and Kathy saying something in the playground this morning about you training AK! Why didn't you tell me about this?' snapped Ray.

AK groaned. He should have trusted his instincts and not mentioned Frank to the girls.

'It's no big deal,' said Frank. 'I'm just giving AK a bit of help.'

'Help?' said Ray bitterly. 'You couldn't help anyone!'

'He is helping,' said AK. 'He knows a lot about running.'

'Why would you help AK when you never help me?' yelled Ray, tears gathering in his eyes. 'What

makes him better than me, eh? How come he gets your attention when you just ignore me or shout at me?'

'It's different,' said Frank. 'This is coaching.'

'I know you don't like me,' AK added, 'but I really need a coach and your dad has some great ideas.'

'I can't believe you've been doing this behind my back!' shouted Ray at his father.

'I was going to tell you,' said Frank.

'No you weren't!' snarled Ray. 'Since Mum left you've just worried about your own troubles and never given me a second thought.'

'I'm going to turn things around.' Frank stepped towards his son. 'Coaching AK has given me a new lease of life. I promise you – '

'Your promises are worth *nothing*!' shouted Ray. 'I hate you!' He shook a fist in his father's face and then turned on his heels and stomped out of the park.

'Wait!' called Frank, hurrying after him.

'Leave me alone!' Ray broke into a run. Frank started running too and a few moments later they were both gone from view.

AK took a very deep breath and blew out his cheeks. This wasn't great. He'd found a coach – albeit one who desperately needed to piece his life back together – he'd got his first race lined up, and now his coach and his coach's son looked like they were on the verge of killing each other. And if Ray had loathed AK before this afternoon, surely things would be far worse from now on? The father who'd obviously shown no interest in his son was now spending loads of time with another kid who'd just arrived in the UK. It was such a mess.

AK waited twenty minutes but Frank didn't return. He did some warm-ups and some press-ups followed by a few laps, but his heart wasn't in it.

***

'How are things going with Mr Tinnison?' asked Dad that night at supper.

'Not bad,' replied AK.

'When do we get to meet him?' asked Mum. 'You know, compare him to Brother Colm?'

'He's really busy,' said AK quickly. 'He has loads of teaching commitments and clubs to run. You might not see him for a while.'

'Oh.' Dad sounded disappointed. He always loved chatting to Brother Colm at athletics events or parents' evenings.

That evening, Perminder and Kathy called for AK and asked if he wanted to go for a walk. He felt a bit angry with them – they were the ones who had led Ray Tinnison to him and Frank – but it wasn't really their fault. He hadn't asked them *not* to talk about it. It was just bad luck that Ray had overheard them.

The three of them spent an hour sitting on a wall by the local fish and chip shop, chatting to people they knew who were going inside, and trying to guess the life stories of the people they didn't know.

'I bet she was a bank robber and stole two million pounds,' said Kathy, pointing at an elderly lady with a sleek greyhound.

'Yeah,' laughed Perminder, 'and all of the money is stored in the dog's kennel!'

Despite his worries, AK couldn't help but laugh.

***

AK felt on edge during school on Wednesday, dreading seeing Ray in school, but he didn't seem to be around.

When AK got to the park after school he was disappointed to find that Frank wasn't there. What had happened yesterday when he'd gone after Ray? Had they had a massive fight? Was one of them lying dead in a gutter somewhere?

As AK waited, he started thinking about Ray's situation. Here was a boy whose mother had left him, and whose father was in a pretty bad way. How must that feel? It was like he'd been deserted twice. And seeing that his dad – who clearly hadn't been around much for Ray – was now spending loads of time with AK must have been like a hammer blow.

A wave of guilt suddenly washed over AK. Maybe he should tell Frank he didn't want to be coached by him any more; that Frank should go and spend some time with his son, build some bridges. All of this pain and heartache must explain why Ray was so aggressive. He was furious with his parents, but since they weren't around, he took his anger out on other people.

AK waited half an hour but Frank still didn't show. AK felt a rising surge of misery as he watched a couple of young women jogging while pushing baby buggies.

How could he take part in Saturday's race if Frank wasn't around, not just to give him extra coaching but to get him into the stadium? Without Frank it would be a write-off.

Maybe Ray was right about his dad. Maybe he was unreliable. Although AK had tried not to get too excited about the race it hadn't been totally possible. He'd experienced an adrenaline rush every time he thought of it. And now he wouldn't get a chance to run.

Why did life have to be like this? You got a really good piece of news and before you knew it, it was totally ruined.

***

On Thursday AK was so distracted in school that Mr Sells called him over after form time to ask if everything was OK.

'I'm fine,' said AK, trying to put on a brave face.

'Are you having problems getting used to life in the school?'

AK shook his head. 'Things are OK. I just miss my friends back home.'

'Of course you do! It's good to see you've hooked up with Kathy and Perminder. They're great kids; they're what we in the teaching profession call characters!'

AK nodded but said nothing further.

He wasn't sure about going to the park after school but he did, worrying on the way about Ray's angry outburst and the possibility that Saturday's race would have to be a no-show. But when he arrived at the park gates he was surprised to see Frank waiting for him.

This wasn't the Frank he'd been training with for the last few weeks. This Frank had ditched the filthy clothes and was now wearing a pair of jogging trousers and a tracksuit top, both clean. His hair was still greasy and matted, though.

'Sorry about the radio silence,' said Frank. 'I had some stuff to sort out at home. I've made some big changes – talked to people, talked to Ray. Listened to Ray. He was right. I've been a total waste of space and I wasn't around for him. I just wallowed in my own dejection and didn't think about how he must have felt. I'm trying hard now to sort things out with him.'

AK was pleased to hear all of this, but he had to ask. 'Am I not doing that race on Saturday, then?'

'Of course you are!' said Frank. 'I know we lost a couple of sessions but we've got today and tomorrow, so we need to get going right now.'

A spark of positive emotion ignited inside AK. Maybe there was still a chance he could get a decent result?

CHAPTER 12

MEETING MUM AND DAD

Thursday's training session went well. Frank ran two full 800-metre circuits with AK, trying to push his student as much as possible. AK beat him easily but it was good to try and create some of the tension he'd be experiencing on Saturday.

On Friday morning AK saw Ray in the playground. Ray gave him a funny look. Was it a look of hate, of bitterness or jealousy? It was impossible to tell. Once again AK thought about Ray and his father's absence, and he felt a tight knot in his stomach.

Friday's running session was less good, as it rained heavily – the first proper downpour AK had experienced since his family's move to London. He did a few warm ups and a bit of running but the path became skiddy and dangerous very quickly.

'Don't worry,' said Frank, as they sheltered under a tree. 'The forecast for tomorrow is excellent.'

After supper that night, AK Skyped Musa again and told him about Saturday's race. This was a mistake because his mum had just wandered into the room.

'You've got a race tomorrow!' she exclaimed.

AK spun round and his heart sank.

'Good luck!' grinned Musa from the computer screen. 'I want a report as soon as it's over! Then I can tell Brother Colm about your famous victory – that'll keep you in the front of his mind for when you come back!'

AK laughed, and soon after the call ended.

'Why didn't you tell us about this race?' demanded his mother.

'I forgot,' said AK meekly.

'Has this Mr Tinnison organized it?'

'Kind of.'

'And if I hadn't just heard you talking about it to Musa I would have never known?'

'I thought you'd be busy,' said AK.

'Too busy to see my own son in his first English race!' cried Mum. 'Are you crazy?'

'Who is crazy?' asked Dad, entering the room.

Mum told him the story and then it was Dad's turn to berate AK for not telling them.

'OK, OK,' said AK, 'you know about it now! You can come and watch me and bring Bibi too.'

'You'd better believe it!' said Mum, making AK write down the name of the stadium and the race times.

AK grabbed an early night and although he was nervous and excited about the race tomorrow, he was fast asleep by 9.45 pm.

***

Saturday dawned with a clump of light grey clouds that faded by mid-morning and gave way to a watery blue sky. After a quick breakfast, AK went to his room to mentally prepare for the race. This was more easily said than done because Bibi kept on putting her head round the bedroom door and wishing him luck.

At 11.15 the family left the flat and caught two buses to the Finn Arena, a purpose-built stadium that had been put up on waste-ground with a big government grant some fifteen years previously.

When they arrived at the stadium there were already a large number of people standing outside chatting or making their way inside. AK initially missed Frank, whose appearance was so changed it was almost impossible to recognize him. Gone was the lank and greasy hair, replaced by a neat short cut. He was clean-shaven, and wearing fawn chinos and a blue button-down shirt.

As AK stood open-mouthed, staring at this remarkable transformation, Frank walked straight over to the family.

'You must be AK's parents,' Frank said, giving them each a firm handshake. 'And I'm assuming this little lady is the famous Bibi.'

Bibi giggled as Frank shook her hand too. Dad put a hand round AK's shoulders. 'You must be Mr Tinnison,' said Mum.

'Please, call me Frank.'

'AK has talked a lot about you,' said Dad. 'We're very grateful for all of the time you've put into helping our son. The school is extremely lucky to have a dedicated running coach like you.'

'I agree!' smiled Mum. 'Putting in all those hours after school is a noble thing to do. I hope they pay you extra!'

'Can we please *not* talk about school?' said AK, who had 'forgotten' to tell his parents about Frank's true status, while also 'forgetting' to tell Frank that his parents thought he was a teacher at Barker Academy. AK knew he would have to tell his parents and Frank the truth at some point but now wasn't the right time.

'I suggest you get changed,' said Frank. 'I'll meet you up in the coaching area. Your family can go through and grab some decent seats.'

There were lots more handshakes and then everyone split up.

AK breathed a sigh of relief and headed off in the direction of a sign that said COMPETITORS. This led inside the building to a short queue, at the front of which sat a bespectacled woman with several sheets of paper and a pen.

When AK reached her she asked him for his name and his race. Once he'd divulged these details she ticked him off her list and produced a white square with the number 80 on it.

'Your number has self-adhesive on the back,' she explained. 'Peel off the corners and stick it to the front of your running shirt. Failure to do so will mean you can't enter your race.'

AK thanked her, took his number and followed the arrows to the boys' changing area. This was a large brightly-lit space with benches round three sides.

There were maybe fifty boys in various stages of getting changed, some already in running gear, some doing up the laces on running shoes, a few just sitting around looking overwhelmed.

AK changed out of his jeans and t-shirt into black running shorts and a white running vest and he carefully attached the number 80 to his chest. He then walked through a door marked TO THE TRACK.

Stepping out was a dramatic experience. The stadium had stands on all four sides and a capacity of five thousand spectators. There were nowhere near that number present today but there were a good few hundred, and to AK it felt like arriving in the Olympics. The track was red and made from polyurethane. One circuit was four hundred metres. AK would have to do two laps for his race. It was all so... so *real*. Soon he'd actually be on the track, running!

AK stood, taking it all in, and then spied Frank calling him over. There were two cordoned-off areas by the start lines marked COACHES and COMPETITORS. Frank was standing in the COACHES area. There were several men and women in suits and tracksuits talking to individual runners or small groups, some with clipboards, some with whistles, all looking earnest and focused.

'Your race is first,' said Frank.

'First!' gasped AK, the nerves jangling wildly in his stomach.

'Apparently the kid you need to look out for in the 800 metres is called Ricky Millet. He's the spindly boy over there. Mike Rivers told me about him.'

AK snatched a glance at a wiry boy about his age and height with long shocks of brown hair. He looked like he'd been assembled from drinking straws.

'Your parents have taken seats on the last bend,' said Frank. 'I saw a couple of girls with them. Your mum said the girls called for you last night after you were in bed and she told them about today's race – said they should pop along.'

Perminder and Kathy! Thanks, Mum.

'Now, remember the things we've done so far, as well as everything you learned back in Kenya. Get that good start, don't allow yourself to go upright, break well, maintain your position and go for the sprint within the last hundred metres, OK?'

AK nodded nervously. 'You look really different,' he said.

'I've made a big effort today. I didn't want to let you down,' said Frank. 'And although I've got a long way to go, I've started to sort a few things out. For the actual race I'll be with your parents.'

Before AK could say anything about this arrangement, there was a booming announcement from the stadium's public address system: *'Competitors for Race One, please move to your starting positions.'*

'That's you,' said Frank. 'Good luck and give it your best shot. Wherever you finish it will be a valuable exercise, OK?'

They shook hands quickly and AK began walking towards the race official – a woman with a blonde bob haircut and a green jacket who was waiting by the 800-metre start lines.

This was it.

Whatever Frank said, doing badly would be a soul-destroying disaster for AK. What was the point of coming sixth when you could come first? He shivered as a breeze rustled past him. Was this going to go all wrong for him? The only way to find out was to run it.

CHAPTER 13

BEATING THE WIND

The race official called out the runners' names and their allotted lanes. AK was given Lane 4 and he walked to his starting line. He spotted Ricky Millet taking his place in Lane 6.

AK closed his eyes.

I am a runner. I have speed. I can beat the wind.

Slowly he opened his eyes and stared down his lane. This was his first race outside Kenya. This was his first race in a far colder climate than that which he was used to. Both facts made him apprehensive. But new experiences didn't have to be bad ones, did they?

He took a quick look again at Ricky. If Frank was right, Ricky was the kid to beat.

'Take your marks!' commanded the official, positioning herself on the side of the track. She held a starting pistol. AK took a very deep breath and blew it out. Around the stands there was chatter and excitement. In unison with Ricky and the other six runners, AK stepped up to his line and positioned himself for the start. Adrenaline whipped through his body.

'Get set!'

Images of Brother Colm, the gleaming red arches of Iten and Musa's grinning face danced through his brain.

BANG!

AK sprung forward, his right foot hitting the track and propelling his body forward.

I am a runner. I have speed. I can beat the wind.

It was a good start, crisp and disciplined. He flew forwards, his arms pumping by his sides, his body parts working in harmony. He overtook the boy in Lane 3 and then the boy in Lane 2. But Ricky Millet had enjoyed an equally good start and was nearly parallel with him. Dust kicked up on the red tracks. The sound of pounding trainers echoed in the afternoon air.

At the bend the runners broke and AK tried not to feel overwhelmed by the importance of this process.

Ricky Millet stole first place and the boy in Lane 7 took second – both went for Lane 1. AK grabbed third place, his right leg in Lane 2, his left in Lane 1, as he had done so many times before. There were to be no heroics, no deviation from the game plan. If Ricky or the other boy had the reserves to pull away and leave AK for dust then that would be what happened. He just had to assume he would have the edge on them in the race's final throes.

Pace for pace AK matched the front two, and in what seemed like a few seconds they reached the halfway mark – four hundred metres, the end of the first lap. With a quick look over his shoulder AK saw that the rest of the pack had fallen six, maybe seven metres behind the front three.

Keep it up, AK told himself. *Whatever you do, do not lose these two guys in front of you!*

On and on AK ran, his mind and body totally focused. Just before the six-hundred-metre mark, Ricky Millet made his move. He obviously believed he had enough power to pull away far enough to prevent anyone else catching him.

AK had been waiting for such a burst of pace but he was surprised by how early it was, and he felt a thud in his chest. Ricky was now sprinting. The boy in second place was not up to it and despite an attempted surge was held back by insufficient reserves of power.

But AK wasn't having it. With every muscle and nerve ending snapping within him, he kicked out and shot forward, passing the second-placed boy and hurtling towards Ricky.

Ricky was clearly well trained at this manoeuvre and had five metres on AK. As they approached the final bend AK was filled with an intense sense of dread that this was to be his fortune; he would have completed a well-paced but ultimately doomed race.

That was when he picked out some familiar faces in the crowd. There were his parents and Bibi, cheering him on. Next to them were Perminder and Kathy, jumping up and down and screaming at the top of their voices. He saw Frank, holding a stopwatch and yelling encouragement, the veins on his neck standing out, determination written all over him. But next to Frank he saw a face that sent waves of electrical shock snapping through him.

It was Ray, pumping his fists in the air and shouting, 'Go, AK!'

Frank and Ray had made up. Something had changed for them.

The sight shifted something within AK. He felt a fiery pulse of energy surging through his body.

I am a runner. I have speed. I can beat the wind.

His legs suddenly started hitting the track at furious speed. He was an out of control train, he was a specially configured racing robot. As Ricky

Millet hit the home straight, assuming the race was his, AK came like a thunderbolt from a hidden cloud, matching Ricky step for step, and then overtaking him in eight paces.

The finish line was now just twenty metres away and the yells of his supporters pushed AK further ahead, opening up daylight between him and Ricky Millet.

The finish line was fast approaching.

AK arched his body, ready to dip his head for a photo finish. But there would be no need for one.

Nothing on earth was going to stop him now.

Airlock
Simon Cheshire

George, Josh and Amira are visiting a space station when a massive explosion destroys almost all of the station, and most of the crew. Trapped in the wreckage, hurtling towards Earth, can George and his friends figure out who's to blame? And will they make it back alive?

ISBN 9781408196878   £4.99

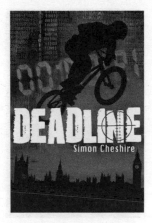

Deadline

Simon Cheshire

When Sam and Karen's mum is dragged away
by armed police, their whole lives change. With
no clues apart from a cryptic message screamed as
she leaves, the kids find themselves in a dangerous
race against time to stop a bomb from exploding
and save their mum's life...

ISBN 9781408131107   £4.99

The Gorgle
Emma Fischel

Finn doesn't want to move to the spooky old house
in the first place. Then he sees the creature that's been
hibernating in this wardrobe. It's a Gorgle. A bit like
a moth, a bit like a hornet, and a lot like a ten-foot-
tall monster from your worst nightmare. It's awake.
It's hungry. And Finn is the only one who can stop it!

ISBN 9781408174135   £4.99